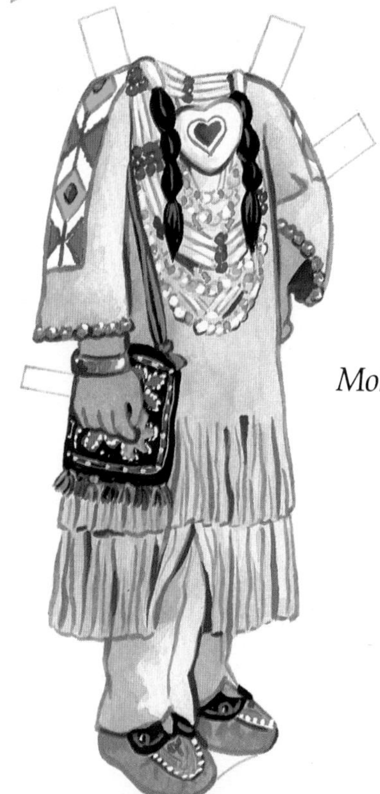

Mohawk

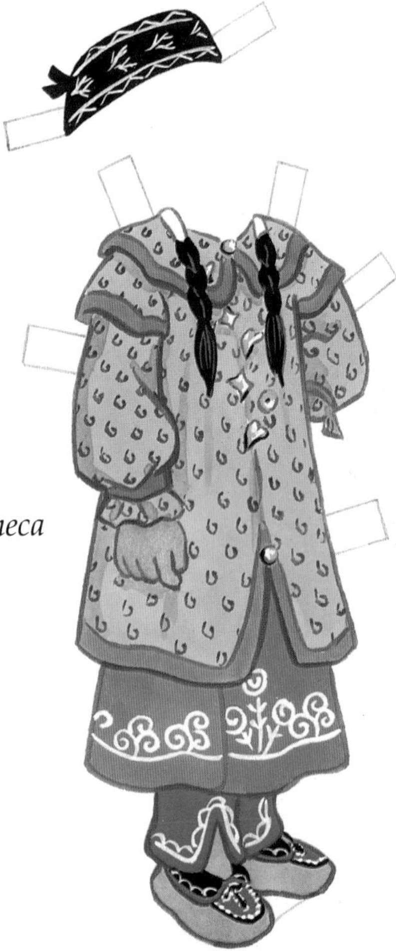

Seneca

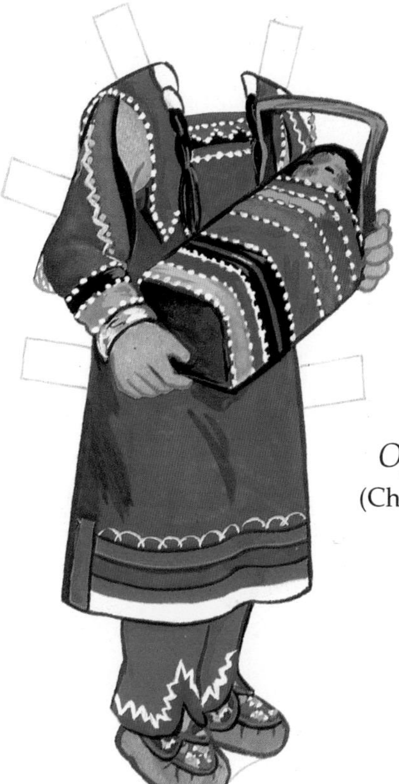

Ojibwa
(Chippewa)

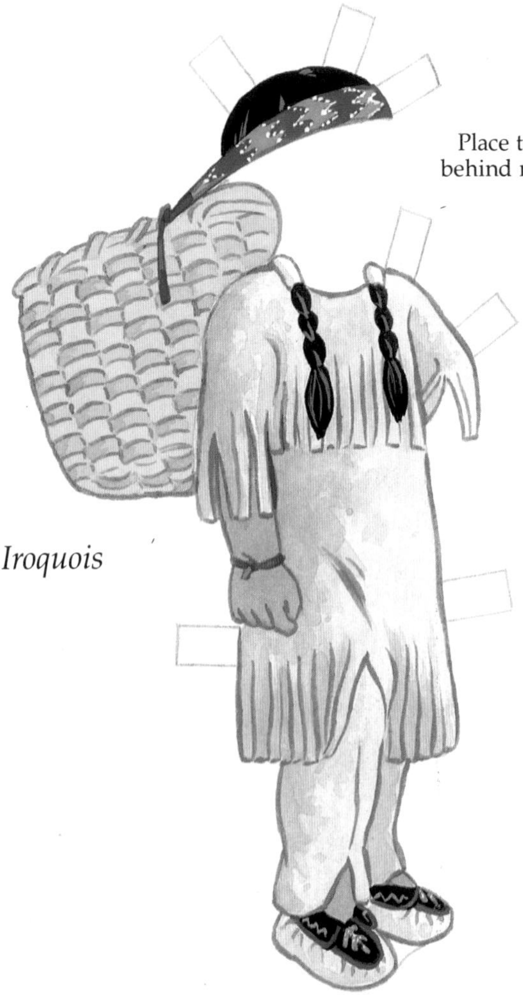
Place tab
behind neck

Iroquois

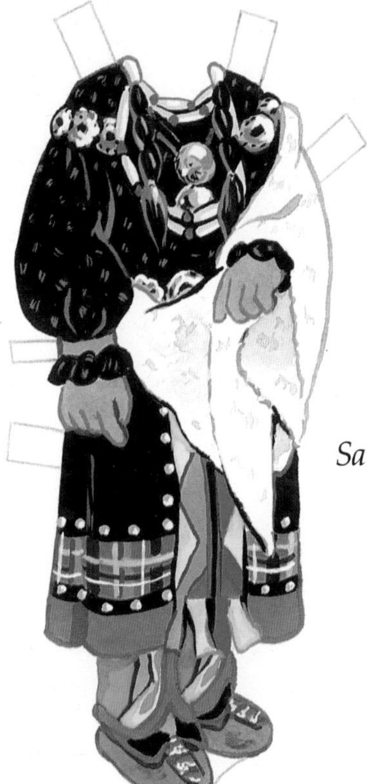

Sauk & Fox

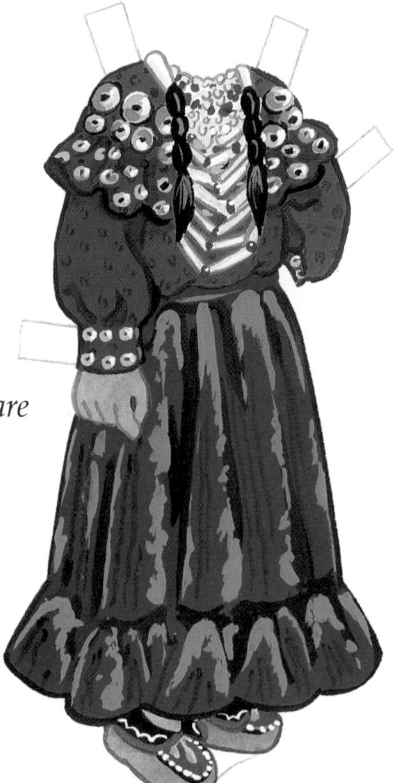

Delaware

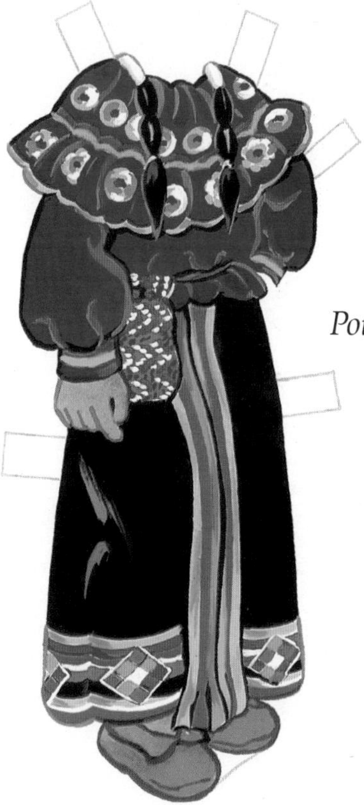

Potawatomi